In memory of my grandparents, Sam & Ida and Ralph & Sayd,
who were always there. —N. L.

For Nancy, up there in the stars. —A. M.

Library of Congress Cataloging-in-Publication Data:

Laden, Nina, author.
Are we there yet? / by Nina Laden ; illustrated by Adam McCauley.
        pages cm
Summary: On the way to grandmother's house, a young child's constant refrain of
"Are we there yet?" turns a boring car trip into an imaginative adventure.
ISBN 978-1-4521-3155-9 (alk. paper)
1. Automobile travel—Juvenile fiction. 2. Humorous stories. [1. Automobile travel—Fiction.
2. Humorous stories.] I. McCauley, Adam, illustrator. II. Title.

        PZ7.L13735Ar 2016
        [E]—dc23
                2015002693

Manufactured in China.

Design by Cynthia Wigginton.
Typeset in CA Postal.
The illustrations in this book were rendered in mixed-media.

10 9 8 7 6 5 4 3 2 1

Chronicle Books LLC
680 Second Street
San Francisco, California 94107

Chronicle Books—we see things differently.
Become part of our community at www.chroniclekids.com.

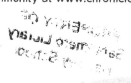

ARE WE THERE YET?

Nina Laden

AND

Adam McCauley

DISCARD

chronicle books · san francisco